To..........Baby..Nichter.........

with a heart
full of love

You are surrounded by so many
family and friends that
love you! You are so
special and beautiful!
H will always be here for
you! Love WKU spirit,
Jag "

Love is all around Kentucky

Copyright © 2016 by Sourcebooks, Inc.
Written by Wendi Silvano
Illustrated by Joanna Czernichowska
Design by Quadrum Solutions (www.quadrumltd.com)

Published by Sourcebooks Jabberwocky, an imprint of Sourcebooks, Inc.
P.O. Box 4410, Naperville, Illinois 60567-4410
(630) 961-3900
Fax: (630) 961-2168
www.sourcebooks.com

Source of Production: Phoenix Color, Hagerstown, Maryland
Date of Production: August 2015
Run Number: 5004410
Printed and bound in the United States of America.
PHC 10 9 8 7 6 5 4 3 2 1

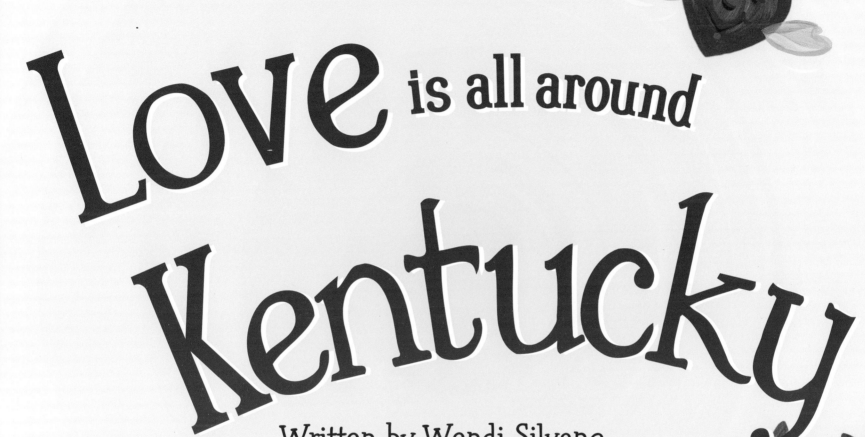

Love is all around Kentucky

Written by Wendi Silvano

Illustrated by Joanna Czernichowska

sourcebooks
jabberwocky

Love is a feeling that comes from **inside.**

Everyone feels it. It can't be denied.

But how do we know that it's there? What's the clue?

How can we **see** it?

Just what can we do?

Love's all around, if you just pay attention,

in people and places too many to mention.

Go look at the **park**,

on the **street**,

at the **mall.**

You'll see love all over. It's **big** and it's small!

All through **Kentucky,** in cars and on trains,
in taxis and buses, on boats and on planes,
in **Louisville, Lexington,**
and **Bowling Green** too,
you'll find there is **love** that will come into view.

BARBARO

Ohio River

Right there, on the lawn, in Jacobson Park

is a **mom** with her **babe,**

hearing songs of a lark.

She **swaddles** him, **cuddles** him,
kisses his ear.

That surely is **love**,
it's perfectly clear!

At a store up in Covington, a girl gets a bear.
She squeezes him,
squishes him,
ruffles his hair.

It's clear that she **loves** him. She's **smiling** and bright.

She tucks him in **softly** and **gently** at night.

That same little girl, the very next day,
sees a **friend** at her school who is too **sad** to play.

So she sits down beside him and **listens** and **shares**,
making sure that he knows there's someone who **cares**.

Now the boy who was **sad** feels much **better**, you see,

so he runs home all happy to play with **Magee**.

They **romp** and they **frolic**.

They **fetch** and they **run**.

It's certain he **loves** him. They're having such **fun**!

You can see how **love** travels

when **shared** with a friend.

If *everyone* shares love, it never will end.

From one to another, it s p r e a d s and it grows.

You can't have *too much*, as everyone knows.

An officer in Richmond who **helps** change a flat.

A fireman in Florence who **rescues** a cat.

RUPP ARENA

The home team that makes the crowd **cheer** and **clap**.
Each moment has **love** like a **gift** you unwrap.

There's a **father** who sits at the table each night,
helping out with the homework to get it just **right**.
He's tired and busy, but that's **love**, you know…
giving up what you want to **help** someone else **grow**.

It's not only *people* who show love, it's true.

Just come see the creatures

that play at the zoo!

The polar bear tumbles

and rolls with her cub,

and when they are finished,

she gives him a rub.

Where else is there love? Have we looked all around?

I think we've forgotten—love grows from the ground!

In the **meadows** and **gardens** and parks you will find

that the earth shows us love of all shapes and all kinds.

Wherever you look, **love** comes into sight.

It's there in the morning, it's there in the night.

But in all of **Kentucky,**

the best love you'll find

is a **love** that is **gentle,**

and **selfless,** and **kind**...

It's the love found at home. It shows up each day
in things people do and in things people say.
There's no greater love, I can tell you, it's true,
than the love of your family...

Especially for YOU!